Sing
a
Song
of
Tuna
Fish

Sing
a
Song
of
Tuna
Fish

A Memoir of My
Fifth-Grade
Year

ESMÉ RAJI CODELL
Illustrations by LeUyen Pham

HYPERION PAPERBACKS FOR CHILDREN/*New York*

Text copyright © 2004 by Esmé Raji Codell
Illustrations copyright © 2004 by LeUyen Pham

For information address Hyperion Books for Children,
114 Fifth Avenue, New York, New York 10011-5690.
First Hyperion Paperback edition, 2006

This book is set in KaatskillH.

1 3 5 7 9 10 8 6 4 2
Printed in the United States of America
Library of Congress Cataloging-in-Publication Data on file.
ISBN 0-7868-5509-6 (tr.)
ISBN 0-7868-3652-0 (pbk.)

Lyrics on p. 50 from "Tune of the Tuna Fish" (from John
W. Schaum Piano Course A—The Red Book), by Wesley Schaum
© 1945 (Renewed 1973) Belwin-Mills Publishing Corp. (ASCAP)
This Edition © 1996 Belwin-Mills Publishing Corp. (ASCAP)
All rights administered by Warner Bros. Publications U.S.
Inc. All rights reserved. Used by permission. Warner
Bros. Publications Inc., Miami, FL 33014

Visit www.hyperionbooksforchildren.com

To Chicago

Contents

Sing a Song of Tuna Fish

INTRODUCTION

Let me tell you something.

When you are a kid, you think you are going to remember everything. You think you are going to remember everyone who sits next to you in class and all the things that crack you up. You think you are going to remember all your favorite foods and toys and the place where you live and all the things that make your family yours, and not the family down the hall or across the street. You think you are going to remember every punishment and big test and rainy day. You think you are going to remember how you feel being a kid. You think you will remember so well that you will be the best grown-up who ever lived.

And you might.

Or you might be like me, who isn't all that old yet but already old enough to get a kind of amnesia. Memories are like days and bones and paper: they can turn to dust, and they change if they are not preserved. Mercifully, a few are

3

packed away. When you're a grown-up, your brain is something like an attic. You have to shove stuff around and dig in some old boxes before you find what you're looking for. That's why if you ask grown-ups for a story, sometimes they have to scratch their heads or pull their chins. They are looking for stories in their attic. Searching in my attic, I found a box marked 1979. After blowing away the dust, I found some memories that survived the passage of time. These are the stories that stuck.

Who knows? Maybe you can use my stories. Maybe they will help you pack your own more carefully, just in case the strange and improbable day should arrive that you forget what it was like to be a child.

Though I hope it never does.

1

The Egg Patrol

Let me tell you something about my mom.

For a while there, she wasn't afraid of burning bridges. That means, she wasn't afraid of making it hard to go back to somewhere she had been. For instance: when my mother quit her job as a waitress, she smashed a ketchup bottle against the wall. "You work so hard for so little money, and then they want something extra," she explained.

Why not burn bridges? Go ahead. If you work hard once, you know you can work hard again, so you don't have to be afraid. But building bridge after bridge to replace the ones you've burned makes a person tired, and a little ornery. My mother worked very hard all her life. After she was a waitress she was a housekeeper; then she settled in to being a secretary, like her own mother. She worked in fancy air-conditioned offices downtown, typing more than a hundred words a minute. Once I went to my mom's office and watched one of her bosses flirt with her.

"I'm going on a business trip, Kitty," he said, even though my mom's name was Betty. "You going to miss me?"

"No," she said. "Not at all."

"Aaww, come on." He sat on her desk. "Tell me that you'll miss me."

"Sure," she said. "I'm great at lying. Come back soon. Don't get in a fiery crash."

He finally gave up.

"Mom, why'd you let him call you Kitty? Why didn't you tell him to . . ."

Mom kept typing and didn't say anything at all, which meant, *Someday you'll know why.* But I didn't worry, because however long Mom bottled things up, sooner or later she would smash that bottle.

The part of Chicago where I lived had been a very fancy neighborhood once upon a time. In the early 1900s, movie studios sprouted up in Uptown; the silent-film star Charlie Chaplin made movies there; and rich people lived among deluxe brick six-flats, department stores, and grand theaters. When I was growing up, there were no more silent movies, and mostly poor people lived in the buildings. But Mom never said *poor*. People in *other* neighborhoods were poor, but people around here were just *broke*. The apartments were crumbling but still spacious, with sagging balconies hanging in front and back, where broke people could sit and relax.

Around eleven o'clock one summer night, I stood on the balcony of our apartment with my mother. A full, yellow moon hung low and easy, leaning on a single cloud. The craters gave the moon a face, looking down upon the same scene as my mother and I. The cool winds off Lake Michigan wrapped my dress around my thin legs. My mother rested against the balcony railing, monitoring some teenage boys walking in the middle of the street. All was serene.

A car came down the street—a shiny red Jaguar. It

parked at the hydrant in front of the public housing high-rise next door. A man got out of the car and strolled into the condominium across the street, where rich people who were waiting for broke people to move out had begun to move in. He carried a six-pack of beer under his arm.

"Schmuck," Mom said, under her breath. "Look at that, how that schmuck parked at the hydrant. What a pig."

"Look at his shiny car," I commented.

"What's wrong with busses?" Mom wanted to know.

"Nothing," I said. "It just looks new. Do you think he's rich?"

"HA!" howled Mom. "Of course he's rich! Do you think a broke person just parks any old place? HA! NO! A *broke* person doesn't even *have* a car! Did you see him strut into that condo with his *beeeeer*?" My mother could not seem to pronounce the name of any alcoholic beverage with anything but contempt.

"What if the high-rise has a fire?" I asked.

"What a joke! I'm laughing! HA! What does he care? As long as he gets a space." I interrupted Mom to pull at her sleeve and point. A police car was coming down the street. It passed the car without slowing. "See? See?" sneered my mom. "He doesn't even get a ticket. Nothing to stop him from doing what he wants. Nothing to show him we don't like it." My mother shook her head. "And I *don't like it.*"

She went into the apartment and came back out again.

With a carton of eggs.

"*Ma!*"

"What? He's a schmuck. The man's a schmuck."

"But *Maaaa!* Gee. You really going to do it?"

"No," she said. She opened the carton and handed me an egg.

"Ma! That's not fair!"

"I'm your mother and you'll do what I tell you," she said plainly. "Now, hit the windshield."

I held the egg in my hand. It was so cold and smooth.

I smiled. Yes, he was a schmuck. Yes, let's bomb him. I looked at the shiny red car from our third-floor porch. Whose boss was *he*? *Hey, Kitty, Kitty.* . . .

"It's pretty far," I pointed out.

"You can do it," said my supportive mother.

"Is anyone around? Is that police car around?" We looked up and down the street. Not a soul in sight.

"Do it," Mom hissed.

I pulled my hand back and flung the egg high into the air. Truly, one of the most beautiful things I have seen in my life was that little ivory missile passing across the moon. It glided through the air so slowly, as though it had wings. Considering it was an egg, it *could* have had wings . . . but we'll never know, because it landed on the hood with a terrible *splursh.*

"Pretty good," said Mom, handing me another egg. "Aim more to the left, go-go-go!"

I looked at my mom in disbelief, and then pitched the egg. The thrill was not gone.

Splirtch.

The egg splattered on the windshield.

"Yay!" My mother cheered and hugged me. "Nice shot."

"Want me to do another one?"

"No." My mother closed the carton. "There are people starving. We don't want to waste."

"Do we have any bacon?" I laughed.

My mother put her arm around me. "We're vigilantes." She sighed, looking down at our work. "We're the egg patrol."

"Mom," I said. "Look at the moon. Doesn't it look like it's staring at us? Like it's *mad* at us?"

My mother nervously looked at the moon. "No," she decided. "It thinks it was a good joke."

"Mom, is this a bad neighborhood?"

"Lots of nuts around here," she said.

"Well, what if that guy gets out of that party really late, and he sees the egg on his windshield and it's all dried up. So he goes back to the party to get paper towels, and while he's wiping up his windshield, some guys come and hold him up and kill him." We were silent.

"Or, what if he doesn't clean his windshield, so he can't see where he's driving and he gets in a crash?"

"*Shvieg*," said my mother. "That won't happen." We gazed down at the egg white, glimmering wet under the streetlight. "He shouldn't park in front of hydrants."

"Well, that one time we did have a car, didn't you get a hundred and twenty dollars in parking tickets?"

"Always talking," said my mother. "You don't know when to stop talking."

I looked up at the moon. No, I was *sure* it was frowning. Its crater eyebrows were all scrunched up with concern and disdain. "I'm going in," I said quietly, and tucked myself into bed. I couldn't stop thinking about the frowning moon.

My mother came into the bedroom and kissed me on my forehead.

"*Maaa!* I feel guilty," I moaned.

"Shhh!" She was grinning. "I feel guilty, too. Wasn't it fun? Don't worry. Tomorrow you'll only feel guilty because you won't feel guilty anymore."

Mom lay down beside me. We were quiet for a while.

"Mom?"

"Uh-huh?"

"When I throw eggs with my children someday, we'll clean up after."

"Oy," said my mother. "That's a good girl."

2
My Neighborhood

Now, let me tell you something about where we lived.

My neighborhood was my world when I was growing up. It was a very cramped world. I did not like to go outside much, because I was scared of things. I did not like to walk around without my father, because a lot of the men were out of work and would sit in their cars and on the stoops and whistle at my mother. There were bars and liquor stores everywhere and people were often fighting. If I was standing alone and waiting at the corner for a public bus, men would pull up and open the passenger side door and there would be money on the seat. My mother had taught me well enough not to get in, but it was still scary and shocking and I had to learn to say no and look mad. When I got off the bus after school, sometimes I felt as though I was being followed, and I would wave up at empty windows to give the impression that someone had their eye on me. In fact, I could not go to the corner grocery store without one of my parents watching me the whole way from our window. My little brother was braver than I was, and rebelled. He played outside and would not always tell my father where he was going. Even when he was very little, he was not afraid of taking dares and getting in fights and playing with matches, if it meant he could make friends. He would be outside all day, playing baseball in the back parking lots. He had a much nicer time, I think.

Here is a tour of some places you would have found in my neighborhood all those years ago. Take my father's hand, and you won't have to be afraid.

WOOLWORTH'S

There was a store that they don't really have anymore; it was what my grandma called "the five and dime," or Woolworth's. Nowadays we have Kmart and Wal-Mart and Target, and Woolworth's was kind of like that, only the stuff was cheaper and easier to reach. They sold lots of everyday things all lined up in aisles: thread and yarn and needles, aprons, hanging plants and silk flowers, greeting cards, and perfumes that smelled like a drunk man's breath. The toys they sold were pretty good: bubbles, dolls as tall as I was, toy cash registers, doctor's kits with candy pills, and bags of little plastic dinosaurs that my brother liked (you could also get army guys or farm animals if you preferred). The best part of Woolworth's was the back of the store, where they kept the live animals, or recently live animals. There were shrieking budgie parakeets, hamsters jogging in wheels, and tanks of snails and goldfish so crowded together they could hardly turn. There was usually a goldfish floating belly up, or flagging on its side with a clouding eye. Sometimes they weren't very well taken care of, but I think that made them tough. We bought a goldfish named Sammy there, and he lived for seven years.

Toward the cashier there were usually Mexican jumping beans rattling inside little plastic boxes with clear covers. I thought they were magic. Holding them in my hand, I could not believe beans could jump, but there was the evidence! Later, someone told me that a tiny worm is in each bean, and when the bean gets warm, the worm wiggles—that's what makes it jump. (I am not sure if this is true, and I don't want to know.) Woolworth's also sold Venus flytraps, which are plants from North Carolina that catch and eat flies. They were fun for a while, but when they did catch a fly, it was kind of gross and I felt bad for the fly, and when they didn't catch a fly they turned brown. It was kind of a lose-lose plant.

As we exited Woolworth's, my father always dug into his pocket for change because there were lots of gumball machines, a little booth with a curtain where you could have your photo taken, and a big mechanical horse that swayed forward and backward. There was also a scale that would give you your weight and your horoscope. I really liked watching the wheel spin to my weight (54 pounds), but I didn't like getting my horoscope. I didn't want to know what would happen next. I'd rather it be a surprise.

DAVIDSON'S BAKERY

Davidson's Bakery had lots of lovely sample cakes in the window. The cakes looked real, but they were made of cardboard and plaster. You could point to one, and the women in white smocks would make one for you out of real cake and frosting. Behind the plate glass you could view cakes with trains on a track, or a baseball field with a batter and a pitcher. There were cakes with storks carrying babies, and cakes shaped like books, overflowing with flowers for first Communions. But I liked the cakes that had a doll on top—a doll with soft hair in finger curls, poised on a heart-shaped stand, with eyes that opened and closed if you tilted it. The doll was surrounded by sugar roses, and I thought that people making roses out of frosting was a miracle. And how did they get the sprinkles around the side of the cake so evenly? I imagined they used some sort of gangster gun that sprayed sprinkles. There were wedding cakes with layers held up by pillars, and one even had a tiny working fountain. I thought it would make a very nice hat.

Cakes were special, though. Usually we got cookies, which the ladies put in a clean white box and tied with twine. My favorites were little cookies with a pink sugar button in the middle. To put one of those on your tongue was like tasting a candy cloud. They had a strange smell, vanilla and confectioner's sugar, which to me was better than perfume. I thought, When I'm a grown-up lady, I hope I can find perfume that smells like these cookies! (I still haven't.)

CURRENCY EXCHANGE

The currency exchange was an important place. My father came here a lot to pay the gas bill and collect food stamps from a man behind the glass who only spoke through a metal grate. My brother and I liked it because there were lots of pens, and forms to fill out. It felt very official. There were lots of posters about energy and utility companies—posters with blue flames and words like "power" and "savings." Or we could go stare at the angry faces of criminals on the "wanted" posters, and see how they would look had they decided to grow a mustache while they were on the lam.

SVEN THE BARBER

Sven's TV was always tuned to *The Price Is Right*. He had a big swordfish hanging over the mirror. There were comic books and magazines with naked ladies. Sven's shop had all sorts of bottles full of sprays and foams, and weird-shaped brushes and combs soaking in turquoise water. There were usually older men in there who weren't even getting a haircut; they were just sitting. Sometimes they didn't even have any hair. Sven liked my dad, and my dad liked Sven, even though when we got on the sidewalk he usually said, "I'll fix it when I get home."

MEL'S

Mel's Diner was a single counter and always open all hours, in the triangular building where Broadway met Clarendon. If I was lucky, my dad would take me in the middle of the night. He would let me ride on his shoulders the whole way. There was usually a blind man there—a regular—he had an even, buzzing voice that sounded like a transistor radio. The men were older and wore jackets even when it was warm, and liked to talk about sports. All the sounds of these men and their deep laughter mixed in with the sounds of the grill, frying and scraping. It was one of the coziest places I ever knew.

I could never understand why the hold-up men shot Mel. I was sure Mel would have just given them the money—everyone was sure—he was always giving away money and food. They didn't have to kill him. All they had to do was ask. But they were never caught, so nobody could tell them so.

The corner got boarded up and abandoned after he died.

Ha-Lo Gift Shop

Ha-Lo was a stationery and office supply store, and I loved the rows of pretty greeting cards, the elegant gold stickers with initials embossed on them, and the crisp letter-writing paper that made me want to make more friends so I could have more letters to write. The woman who ran the store wore glasses and her hair in a bun, and was sometimes friendly, sometimes not. The Ha-Lo Gift Shop had a mystery surprise in it. It had a secret basement room. You needed a parent with you to go in. When my birthday was coming, the woman would turn on the light and my mother and I would follow her down the wide flight of stairs, where there were party supplies and an Aladdin's cave of party favors. My mother held out a big plastic basket and we would pick packet after packet of kazoos, notepads, necklaces and bracelets, toy cars, rubber snakes, whistles, stickers, pencil sharpeners, fake money, tiny games where you roll ball bearings into holes . . . everything, everything a kid could ever want in a goody bag. We would pick out streamers and blowers and funny hats. My mother never said no to anything. If I even looked at something in that basement, she read my face and threw it in the basket. By the time we left, our fingers were pinched with the weight of the shopping bags, and my heart was just as full. It is wonderful to be spoiled as a child.

THE LAUNDROMAT

I think I spent about a third of my childhood in the Laundromat. I never liked the word "boring," even as a child, but I have to say I thought it was the most boring place ever. The highlight was putting the coins in the washers and dryers, or getting coins from the change machine. Sometimes my brother and I could push each other in the carts, but generally this was frowned upon. Usually, we would stare at the washer and count up to a number and see if the cycle was done by that number, even though it usually wasn't. We were luckier than most, because our parents would take us for a walk during the wash cycle and sometimes we would get McDonald's. Most people didn't dare leave their laundry, because someone might steal it. There were usually a lot of kids in the Laundromat, but as often as not we didn't speak the same language, so you had to play quiet, pointless games like rock-paper-scissors. Some families brought in so much laundry, it was amazing. They heaved endless boulders of dirty clothes and had to be there forever. When the washing and drying were done, then came the folding, folding, folding, the endless folding. If you forgot something to read, you were out of luck, because then you just had to meditate or read the religious pamphlets left on the plastic chairs, which all said the same thing: you were going to hell. I didn't worry too much about it, though. Hell was probably a Laundromat, and I was already managing to survive.

Bus Stops

After Laundromats, we spent the most time waiting at bus stops. My father didn't drive. He felt all these cars interfered with man's ability to think and write poetry, which was too high a cost for just getting somewhere. My mother felt having a car was too high a cost, period, so we took busses everywhere. If I waited for a bus with my mother it was no problem, because she had a trick. She would light a cigarette, and a bus would come almost immediately. But since my father didn't smoke, he had to wait a long time for his busses to come. The more urgent it was that we get somewhere, the more likely it was that we would miss our bus by a nanosecond. We would wait in all kinds of weather, and my father would start out very optimistically, saying another bus was sure to follow very soon. But after a while, he would start pacing and stepping off the curb into the street and squinting his eyes. After a while longer than that, he would start swearing. After a while longer than that, he would start talking about government conspiracies against him. And after a while longer than that, he would start talking about my mother's role in government conspiracies against him. And if (Heaven help us) we passed the forty-five-minute mark and the bus still had not come, my father would start railing in a complicated tongue that was unknown to anyone except for him and the man who talked to the mailbox. He would start foaming at the corners of his mouth, and anyone else who was waiting would decide to take a little walk to the next stop. When the bus finally came, there were always three in a row, and it was all he could do to keep from flinging the change in the driver's face. Then we would sit down and he would sigh a big sigh and smile a big smile and wipe the froth from the corners of his lips and say, "See, I told you it would come."

Waveland Bowl

My father liked to take us bowling. Sometimes our mailman went with us—he liked to bowl, too. We would tie on the floppy two-toned shoes and cheer away an afternoon. Nowadays bowling alleys are automated, but back then the man would give you a score sheet and a short pencil with no eraser to keep track. This meant you could take a lot of practice rolls. Whatever score we got, my dad would tell us that it was very good for our age. My brother still got frustrated by his score.

Waveland Bowl had a great soda machine that didn't

just drop cans. Instead, a cup would fall down a chute and sit while two streams poured into it, the flavoring and the seltzer. I would always choose black cherry. My father always chose with some ceremony, because he confessed it had been his dream since childhood to get two flavors at once. So he always tried to press two buttons at the same time. It never worked.

TWO DIFFICULT STORES

There were two tiny stores on the same street. One was the cigar store on the corner. The entire window was filled, top to bottom, with junk kids like: yo-yos and cap guns and fashion dolls in bathing suits, and tons of gags like whoopee cushions and black gum and invisible ink. It seemed like everything they had was wrapped in plastic and attached to a colorful piece of cardboard. When you went in, the store was so small you could hardly move— it was more like a hallway than a store. You had to say "excuse me" to turn around, and if someone at the end of the store opposite the door wanted to leave, everyone had to back out onto the sidewalk to make room. Everything was attached to the wall; you had to tell the man what you wanted and he'd get it for you from behind the counter. The cigar store also sold candy. My brother liked to get a Lik-a-Stik, which was a block of hard sugar that you would lick and then dip into packs of different flavored loose sugar. Besides an occasional licorice pipe, I usually didn't get any candy there. It was enough to watch my brother after he ate his Lik-a-Stik. He would run around so fast it looked like a camera trick.

The other little store sold war memorabilia. We did not usually go in that store. Flags with swastikas were displayed in the window, along with lighters, harmonicas, knives in sheathes, and lots of jagged metal things that seemed to be for throwing at people. It was kitty-corner to a restaurant chain called IHOP, the International House of Pancakes, so my father called the store IHON, which was short for the International House of Nazis. Walking in the door felt like walking inside an old black-and-white movie. Everything was gray and smoky and covered with a layer of lint. I would pull my shoulders and arms as close to my body as I could so I wouldn't get dusty. It felt so scary in there and smelled so bad, like the inside of a boot. The men in there would look at me, but never greeted me. My father would pay for his saxophone reeds or shoelaces and we would leave. I would have bad dreams about that store, and sometimes I couldn't even look in the window. What do people want to remember war for? I wondered. I was glad when they closed down.

THE BASKETBALL COURT

Chicago is very green, as far as cities go; you will come across a public park every few blocks. Through most any open window in the warmer months, you can smell lighter fluid and chicken on the grill, or hear the cheers and groans of a crowd enjoying some sport. Once I walked too close to a baseball field, and a line-drive foul gave me a black eye. After that I took to wearing a fluorescent green Oakland A's batting helmet wherever I went. The Chicago Cubs played about a mile from my house, but the Oakland A's were owned by Charley Finley, who invented the orange baseball—which, by the way, you can see coming much more easily than a white baseball if you happen to be walking in a park.

The park near our home also had a basketball court, where my brother and I would watch my father play. The sound of the ball against the sidewalk as my father dribbled sang its high note into the air again and again, and my father would snap his gum with every step. He was usually the only white man playing, and since my father's name was Barry, all the other men would call him "Rick Barry," after a famous basketball player who was also usually the only white guy on the court. The real Rick Barry had a funny technique of shooting free throws underhand from between his legs, like a little girl, and whenever my father went to the line he imitated him and made everyone laugh. It was wonderful to watch the men come to the net all at once, brown arms gathering underneath like stems reaching up for the same orange flower.

The Magic Sidewalk

The concrete in the sidewalk outside the free clinic had some sort of sparkling rock mixed in. On a sunny day, it glinted like diamonds, truly like diamonds, changing brightly in the light. It was very strange and wonderful. I asked my father, what makes the sidewalk twinkle like that? He told us that men went into outer space and got a star and ground it up to make that sidewalk. I wondered at how valuable it must be. Why would the government give people like us the star? I thought they must not have been paying very good attention, putting the star sidewalk right across the street from the liquor store, along a wall that gangs had spray painted with upside down pitchforks and scribbled names. Poor star. Lucky us.

My six-year-old brother would walk so slowly on that sidewalk, being dazzled. "Oh, come *on!*" I hollered one day. "It's *hot!*" My father took my hand and said gently, "We have to be very patient because he is a little boy and he hasn't been on Earth very long. Everything is new to him and he needs to look." So I would hold my father's hand and sigh, and watch my brother walk so slowly, getting used to the planet.

3

A Different Kind
of Schooling

Let me tell you something about education.

My mom and dad did not seem to care much for school. "A in school, F in life," they said more than once. They were always looking for a reason not to send me. I noticed this even on my first day of kindergarten. At snack time, the teacher passed around a basket of cookies. I took two, and she corrected me: "eh-eh-*ehhh*, only *one* cookie, Esmé." After school my mother asked me how it went, and when I came to the cookie part, my mother grew very angry. "Who ever heard of just one cookie for a five-year-old girl? It's *unnatural!* One cookie per hand, at least! Anyone knows *that!* And after what my grandparents went through to get here . . . ! Well, you don't have to go back if you don't want to!" And I didn't especially want to, so I didn't have to.

When I was old enough so that I had to, my parents

went to great expense to send me to a school where you only did what you wanted. My mother would pack me a lunch and take me on the public bus. Most of the other kids were white, and had parents who were lawyers or architects or in advertising, or were poets or sculptors. Most of the parents had money and lived in houses, but you couldn't tell by looking at the kids. The parents let the kids dress themselves, so they usually wore their Halloween costumes or clothes that didn't match, or they wore the same thing every day. If it was hot, sometimes the kids didn't wear anything at all. Some of the children had names like "Space" and "Dawn." The kids were between six and sixteen years old. There were no report cards. We did not sit at desks, we sat on sofas. Each morning you simply wrote your name on sign-up sheets for activities that interested you, then participated in them over the course of the day. There was a little math and reading that you had to do, but for the most part, you could take classes in things like roller skating and disco dancing, or making puppets. Or you could construct a geodesic dome, or sing songs with a lady and her guitar. Or mulch a garden. Or sit with a group and roll peanut-butter balls in granola. Or read a book about how babies are made. Or throw a bowl on the pottery wheel. Or write letters to senators. Or use the mimeograph machine to make a school newspaper. Or crank ice cream. If you had something better to do than all of that, you could go do that, too. Sometimes I went off by myself and wrote plays, and then I made a sign-up sheet for people who wanted to act in them, and so occasionally the whole school would put on my shows.

It was an interesting school, and I learned a lot of things I would not have learned otherwise, but it was a little wild, too. One girl had a pet rat, and she was allowed to bring it to school. It would sit on her shoulder all day. It had a tail like a worm and eyes the color of blood, and sometimes it would urinate on her shoulder. I thought it was the most terrible and evil thing in the world and I could not believe the grown-ups kept letting her bring it.

Another not-so-nice thing I learned at that school was that when grown-ups act like everything's okay with them when it really is not, eventually they explode. Not like a bomb, exactly, but a little like a bomb. For instance, the children would argue with the teachers all the time, and talk back. The teachers wouldn't say anything about it for weeks, but then every so often one of the teachers would scream and even hit a child, and then everyone in the whole school would have to get in a circle and we'd talk about our feelings. I did not tell my parents about the rat, or the hitting, or the children not having to wear clothes. I didn't know my school was different from other schools, so when they asked me how my day was, I would say, "the usual," or show them something I had written during my "choice time."

Things started to change in my family. My little brother started school, and my father needed a job. It was hard to make payments to the school, so my father came to offer social studies for a while and get a price break. When he saw what was going on, he decided to run a very different program. He *made* everyone come to his class, and everyone did, because being told to do something was so different and new. He put tables and chairs in his room and he wouldn't let us sit on the sofas that were there. He read Mark Twain's *Huckleberry Finn* and Anne Frank's *Diary of a Young Girl* aloud to us. He made us study about men like Hubert Humphrey and Vasco da Gama, and we had to write reports. The beginning of the end happened when he told parents he was taking a group of us on a field trip. He brought all of his favorite students over to our apartment on the public bus, and we all ate boiled hot dogs and watched the Chicago White Sox play their opening game on TV. That was fun. My father was fired shortly after that.

My father and mother liked us to stay home anyway; they felt we learned at least as much by watching old movies and by doing our own projects. We did keep busy. My brother liked to look at his baseball cards and play video games, which had just been invented. I liked to dance and read comic books. You may wonder, what was it like to have a mom and dad who are happy when you do not go to school? What do you think? It was wonderful. But hard, too, because in the *Little Lulu* comic books I read, the girl had a very kind teacher named Miss Feeny and everyone sat in desks and did the same thing at the same time. I realized that maybe not every school was like the school I had attended. I thought how nice it would be to have my own desk filled with books, and a person trying to tell me new things all day long. It seemed like a very organized and fancy arrangement.

Once the dust settled, my mom and dad gave up trying to find another private school for me. They sent me to the neighborhood school. As soon as I walked into the building, I could smell amazing smells of cheese and tomato sauce and paint and wood, all mixed together. There were separate bathrooms for boys and girls. When I walked through the polished halls, my shoes made a clean *click, click* sound. There was a little courtyard in the middle of the school with a tree with leaves falling, and a bench—you could see it through big glass windows that reached down to the floor. And then, I went into my classroom. My new teacher, Mrs. Schultz, had jet-black hair and wore a straight skirt and heels and pearls, just like Miss Feeny in the *Little Lulu* comic books. She had the stretchiest smile I had ever seen, and her teeth were so white and wide that there seemed to be rows of little smiles inside her big smile. But the best thing about her was her voice. She didn't talk like me. Every word she said had a cheerful bounce to it, like she was chewing gum while she spoke. I found out later she was from Brooklyn and had a New York accent.

She gave me my desk and she gave me my books, and I got to sit with other little girls, who had pretty names like Amelia and Ruby and Josefina. Everyone was all different colors and wore all different kinds of clothes, but they all sat straight in their chairs and seemed to know just what to do when the teacher passed out long strips of paper. The girl sitting next to me whispered and told me to number my paper one to twenty, and then try to spell the words. At ten years old, I was taking my first spelling test. I couldn't believe that when the teacher said the word, nobody announced that they didn't feel like writing the word, everyone just wrote it and kept their eyes on their paper. One boy raised his hand and said, "how do you spell it?" and everyone laughed at the same time, too. *This is the most organized place in the world!* I thought. At lunch, I stood in line and a lady gave me a warm tray of spaghetti with cheese and a whole box of chocolate milk. The cafeteria doubled as a library, so I ate surrounded by books. Some girls gave me cookies because I was new. When we returned from lunch, the slips of paper were handed back. The teacher had written 100%! *Good job!* across the top, and had drawn a smiley face. Then the teacher went on to talk all about the different climates in different parts of the United States.

I was sure I had died and gone to heaven.

Now, even though my parents didn't care much for

school, they cared a lot about learning. Especially when it came to music. We had a grand piano in our apartment, only it wasn't so grand anymore. It had been a wedding gift to my parents. My mother put plants on it and sometimes she overwatered them and the moisture made the wood peel. When she saw what she had done, she cried, but then I guess she figured what the heck, because the plants stayed there. When I was a very little girl I had written the names of the notes on the keys, using Magic Marker, which didn't help matters. All of this poor treatment was overseen by a heavy bust of Beethoven, who himself suffered from a chipped nose. But the piano still had a fine tone, and my father enjoyed playing from three songbooks in particular: *The Jerome Kern Songbook*, *The Cole Porter Songbook*, and *The Rodgers and Hammerstein Songbook*. He said these composers lived on Tin Pan Alley in New York, along with George Gershwin, who wrote the great concerto *An American in Paris* and whose name was spoken with as much reverence in my household as God. I could just imagine these men, eating cans of baked beans from their tin pans, and then going back to work on their songs on grand pianos covered with plants, poking out oh-sweet-and-love-ly-la-dy-be-good on the keys.

When my mother and brother were out of the apartment, my father and I would skibble over to the piano like mice who are about to play while the cat is away and have a private sing-along. I don't know why we wouldn't do this when other people were around— maybe he was as self-conscious about playing the piano as I was about singing. At any rate, it was something we kept between us. My father liked me to sing a song that went "My heart belongs to daddy, so I simply couldn't be bad." He also liked to pretend he was Donald O'Connor and I pretended I was Ethel Merman, and we would sing a duet called "Just in Love," about a guy who thinks he needs to go to a psychiatrist because he is seeing and hearing and smelling things nobody else can see, hear, or smell, but an older, experienced woman consoles him by saying he's not sick, he's just in love. Even now, I can do a pretty good imitation of Ethel

Merman. Which is too bad, because most people nowadays don't know who Ethel Merman is.

Besides sing-alongs with my dad, my favorite thing to do in life was listen to records. Records are like CD's—they are flat and round and play music—but records are much bigger and made of black vinyl with a hole in the middle. They have to be played on a record player, a spinning turntable on which you lay a long arm at the edge of the record, and a tiny needle runs against a groove in the record to make the music happen. The needle follows the groove round and round and round, until all the music plays itself out, and then at the end you can hear the needle like a tired heartbeat thump, thump, thumping against the label. When you flick the repeat switch, an invisible hand lifts the arm and places the needle perfectly back at the start of the record. I thought the technology was simply amazing.

My parents had hundreds of records in their collection, with plenty of Motown, rock and roll, Broadway show tunes, and jazz. They never made us put the records away in their paper album covers, and some of the covers were missing. I think if they had been sticklers for tidiness, I would not have liked music so much, because part of the fun was switching records about every two minutes, tossing off the needle with a ripping sound the moment a song grew tiresome. Unfortunately, by not putting away the records, they became scratched and warped and sometimes skipped when we played them. My brother and I memorized the skips, so when we came to that part we would just say the words over and over until one of us shoved the needle farther along on the record ("I wanna/I wanna/I wanna/I wanna/hold your hand"). Another technique was to balance coins on the head of the needle so that when it came to a scratch, the needle was weighed down enough to ride over it.

When we played records, my brother liked to stand on the corner of the couch and play air guitar. He had a very original technique, making a crook in his arm and a stroking motion with his other hand, kind of like a robot comforting a baby. He was a good singer, and sometimes I would stand on the opposite corner of the sofa and be his air drummer and backup. This would irritate him very much and he asked that if I was in his band, could I please lip-synch.

Despite my love for music, I had no real desire to learn how to play any instrument. Unfortunately, the down-stairs neighbor directly below us gave piano lessons. Every Monday my father would give me five dollars, my music books and metronome, and I would knock on her door. So began the longest half hour of my week.

Maria had a statue of Jesus on the cross hanging over the piano. He had nails in his hands and feet, and a crown of thorns on his head. He was bleeding painted blood, looking as sad as he could be. I asked my dad who he was, and he said, "a very famous rabbi that the Romans nailed to the cross a long time ago." I knew a little about this because I lived near a church that had a big billboard you could see for blocks that said CHRIST DIED FOR YOUR SINS. There was also a "Joyeria," or

Spanish jewelry store with lots of statues of Jesus's mother, Mary, in the window, who did not look much happier than Jesus did. What really got me about Jesus on the cross were the nails. I did not know much about hardware, but I did know how to get a nail out of a wall, and I felt pretty sure that if I saw a nail in someone's foot, I would use the backside of a hammer and take it out. I could not understand this at all, why everyone stood around while Jesus had nails in his hands and feet. Obviously somebody had a hammer to nail him in. Didn't anyone have a hammer to take him out? And as if being nailed to a cross wasn't enough, he was posted right over the piano and had to listen to children practice. It seemed like adding insult to injury. The whole thing made me so mad. Sometimes I would not hear what Maria was saying to me, I was so busy fantasizing about taking Jesus off that wall and letting him rest in my nice, quiet doll buggy.

Maria had a bottom that was like a king-sized pillow, so I just had a little corner of the bench. She would spend the first ten minutes of the lesson complaining about all the things the landlady needed to fix in our building. She would ask me if I practiced, which was not a fair question, because since she lived right below us she could hear whether I had or hadn't. Then she would open my music book, *The John Schaum Blue Book*. Now that I am a grown-up, I am sure that Mr. Schaum is a perfectly lovely man, but when I was ten years old I used to write him short hate letters, suggesting that maybe he go back to Tin Pan Alley and take some lessons himself. Luckily, I did not know where to mail them.

Maria would demonstrate the piece, which would go something like this:

TU-na fish, TU-na fish,
Sing a song of TU-NA-FISH!
TU-na fish, oh, TU-na fish,
It's a FAV-rite dish!
Ev-ery-bo-dee-loves it SOOO,
From New York to KO-KO-MOOO . . .

My little secret was that even after a year of lessons, I could not read a note of music. I would just watch Maria's hands so carefully, and then when it was my turn, I would copy her movements and follow by ear, just looking up at the music from time to time so it looked like I knew what I was doing.

Another problem was that sometimes I could not understand what Maria was trying to tell me. She was from Cuba and did not speak English very well. She had her own way of pronouncing things. "Stacka-TOE! Stacka-TOE!" she would shout into my ear and mash my fingers harshly against the keys. I was a grown-up before I understood she was trying to tell me to play the notes "staccato," or in a short, jumpy way.

So many misunderstandings! Did the billboard say "Christ died *for* our sins," or "*from* our sins?" I wasn't sure. Jesus's eyes looked like they were rolling.

My best friend at school was a girl named Akila. She had brown skin and black braids and wore a red dot in the middle of her forehead. She had calm eyes and a steady line of a mouth. She was very smart. She was so smart, Mrs. Schultz let her help grade the math papers. This happened to be the way we became friends. One day while we were in line for lunch, she tapped me on my shoulder.

"Oh, Esmé, you are so terrible at maths," she said.

"I know," I said. And I did know. I hardly ever chose math at my old school. So now the other children in the class were doing multiplication and division, while I was still rushing to get the hang of place value. Still, I did not think it was very nice of her to mention it.

"You get more wrong than you get right on almost every test."

"I *know*," I repeated.

"If you don't learn your maths soon, you will get a very bad grade on your report card," she pointed out.

"It's not 'maths,' it's *math*," I said. "And I KNOW."

"Why don't you let me tutor you?" she said. "I'll show you how to do it. It's not so hard."

I had to admit, it was a very kind offer, and after a couple more bad grades I took her up on it. She lived in the high-rise right next to my building. Usually her parents weren't home, just her sister, who was in eighth grade. Her sister rubbed pomade in her hair to make it shiny, and it smelled so powerfully like rancid olive oil that I almost choked every time she greeted me. She also had the worst teeth I had ever seen—it was as if someone had put them in upside down. But she was so friendly and motherly that within a minute or two it was easy to forget these things about her outsides and see her as the rare kind of attractive that only comes from a gentle heart.

Sometimes Akila and I would work on our homework and snack on candy-covered pieces of anise. Other times Akila would show me the makeup kit she used to paint her bindis, the dots she wore on her forehead. She told me that if she had not come to this country, she would have been married by now. She was eleven years old, so I thought she was kidding, but she assured me that she wasn't. She said her parents snuck her and her sister out of their village in India in the middle of the night and came here so they could get an education. It was the first time I realized every child in the world doesn't get to go to school, and that to go to a nice school like I did was even more special than I had ever believed.

Akila and I walked to and from school together. One Monday, I told Akila how much I didn't like piano lessons and what a waste of time they were because after a whole year I couldn't read music, and I would never be able to because there was too much math. Akila, who had been trying to help me with my math for weeks, knew this was probably true and took my complaint seriously.

"You're right," she said. "It is a waste. But what can you do?"

"I wish I just had this one week off," I said. "Then we could play." We stood in the middle of the sidewalk and tried to think of a plan, our breath escaping from us in little clouds. "I know," I said. "You can beat me up."

"What! I don't want to get in trouble!"

"I won't tell on you," I promised. "Just hurt me a little."

"No," she refused. "I've never beat anyone up before."

"Then you should learn," I said, "so you'll be good at it in case you need it."

Akila was a very practical girl. "All right," she said. She hit my arms and kicked me a few times, but it wasn't enough to keep me home from piano lessons.

"You're not making a dent," I accused. "My little brother hits harder. You're not trying."

"I am," she insisted, "but when I have seen kids get hurt, they weren't standing so still. I think you have to fight, too. Create resistance."

"I can't fight you," I said.

"You can't do maths, either," she said. "Stupid."

So I lunged at her and we wrestled to the sidewalk. I struggled on my back while she pulled off her mitten and raised a fist and split my lip. She gasped and stood up. I gasped, too, and put my hand to my mouth and tasted salt. Then I smiled at her.

"I did it!" she cheered, bouncing up and down on her toes.

"Hurry!" I said. "We've got to get home while I'm still bleeding."

We ran to my apartment and I burst through the door, crying. My father came running. "What happened!"

"Some bad boys beat me up," I wept. "Ow!"

My father wiped my face with a washcloth. "You have to go home now, Akila."

"Can't she stay?"

"You have piano lessons today."

"But Dad! My *lip*!" I wailed.

"You don't play piano with your lip, do you?" He handed me five dollars, my music books, and metronome. Akila looked very sorry.

I owed that girl a lot of favors.

4

It Snowed and It Snowed and It Snowed

Let me tell you something about the weather.

Weather in Chicago was very dramatic. In the spring we would have such violent thunderstorms that the clouds seemed to be boiling, and lightning would slice like silver knives across every corner of the sky. Huge explosions of thunder would send dogs whimpering under beds and car alarms wailing, and would blow out all the electricity for hours, leaving us to look for each other in the ghostly strobes of the lightning flashes. Sometimes the wind gusted so hard that umbrellas turned inside out and people would stop and hang on to lampposts to keep from falling down.

The summers blistered us, and the street filled with people on stoops, and the endless noise of double-Dutch chants, ice cream truck jingles, gang whistles, firecrackers, music playing loudly from cars, and women calling for help. The hydrant was opened, and children covered with mosquito bites and sunburn screamed with relief.

The winters were as brutal as the summers. The frozen winds made it feel like you were having a heart attack just walking down the street. On a cold day in Chicago, even your eyeballs are cold. But no winter was colder than the one when I was ten years old in 1979.

The only way I can describe it is to say that it snowed and it snowed and it snowed and it snowed. It snowed until it was as high as the cars, and then it snowed some more, until nobody could find their cars. It snowed until the tops of trees looked like little white bushes coming out of the sidewalk. It snowed until, when they cleared the sidewalk, it was like walking down a white hallway, like Moses crossing a frozen, parted sea. And then it snowed some more.

Everything closed down because some people could not even get out of their doors, and even if they could, nobody could figure out where the sidewalk ended and the street began. This meant snow days from school. The apartment grew darker and darker as the fans of frost spread in layers across the windows, turning them into panes of ice that burned to the touch and trembled against the low, angry moaning of the wind outside. The radiators clanged. It was so cold, even our stingy landlady had to turn on the heat. To keep it off would have been murder.

Finally, after several days and nights, the snowing and the blowing subsided, and my brother and I put on all of our winter layers and got our sled out of the closet. It is a funny thing to have a sled in Chicago, because it is a very flat place where "sledding" usually means "pulling." We bounded out our door and did not even have to go down the flight of stairs to the sidewalk, because the stairs had disappeared and it seemed as if the sidewalk had risen up to meet us.

"Yay!" We cheered, and ran out onto our new, white street. "Yay! Yay! Yay! Yay!"

Suddenly, I realized I was the only one saying "yay,"

and my brother was saying "hey." I turned around. Where was my brother?

I took a few steps back toward the house and saw a round hole in the snow. I saw my brother's surprised face looking up at me. He had fallen through the snow.

I lay on my belly and reached my arm into the hole. He grabbed it and climbed out. We played for a little while, but not very long. It is too scary to play on top of snow that can swallow you up.

The snow didn't melt. Life went on, but at a much slower pace. We teetered to school along the drifts by gripping on to the tops of fences that surrounded buildings. Teachers stopped marking us late.

One day at school, my teacher asked me to deliver a note to another teacher who was in a "mobile" classroom out in the schoolyard. (The school had run out of room for all the children, so some classes were held in little trailers outside of the main building.) I had to get dressed with my coat and hat and boots and such, just to deliver this note. It had been snowing all morning, so when I got outside, the entire playground was dazzling, sparkling like a placid sea. A pathway had been cleared, but I didn't take it. Instead, I climbed up the drifts, getting a secret thrill from making the first line of footsteps. To mar something so perfect felt like mischief, like swiping a finger across frosting on a birthday cake. There were several mobile classrooms, but the icicles were hanging so low over the doors that I couldn't make out the room numbers. I started walking toward one of the trailers, but the snow around my feet seemed to cave in. I jumped gingerly back a few steps and hung on to the gutter of one of the trailers. I knocked on the window, but the classroom was dark. There was snow piled against the door. This trailer was abandoned and empty. They must have moved the classes to the trailers nearer to the cleared path, it occurred to me. Or maybe they were moved inside the main building. *Maybe nobody is out here at all.*

I looked around and realized I was surrounded by snow. I ventured another step and heard a strange icy cracking, like a muffled zipper being pulled in a crooked line somewhere below the glinting white surface. It was at least a dozen steps to the next half-buried trailer. Would the world beneath me unzip? I thought of my brother. But who would pull me out? Was it possible to drown in snow?

I clung to the gutter more desperately, cracking icicles that dropped straight down and made perfect holes like bullets where they fell.

Then I heard a door slam. "Esmé!" called a voice, but I couldn't see anyone. Then a knitted red hat with pom-poms appeared at the edge of the drift. Akila. I breathed again and felt the flat, biting cold fill my lungs. I could only see the top of her head, as she was standing on the cleared path around the school. "Mrs. Schultz sent me to check on you. You were taking so long. Oh!" Akila took in my predicament and her eyes grew round. "How can you tell which is what!"

"I can't," I called.

"Then you'd better come back," Akila said sensibly.

"I can't do that either," I explained. "The snow's too soft. I'll fall and disappear."

"Well, then, how did you get all the way there?"

"Luck," I guessed, even though I did not feel very lucky.

Akila climbed onto the drift. "If you fall, I will pull you out." Before I could stop her, she steadied herself and stepped out toward me. Her leg disappeared to her knee and she teetered forward and gave a strange little bark. "Ahhh!" She pulled her leg out with both hands and stumbled back to the clear path. "That's not going to work. It's like quicksand," said Akila.

"I don't know what to do," I said. My face hurt—even my eyelashes seemed cold. I could no longer feel my toes, and my hand was cramped around Mrs. Schultz's note. We stood in silence.

"I'm sorry I punched you in the face that time," called Akila. "And I'm sorry I said you were bad at maths."

"I *am* bad at math."

"But I'm sorry I said so," she said.

"Please stop talking like that," I said. "I'm not going to be out here *forever*."

Akila didn't say anything. For some reason, that made me shriek in terror. "Ahhhhh!"

Akila brightened. "That's a good idea! AHHHH!"

"AaaAAAAAHHHH!" We both yelled.

A window slammed open. "For Pete's sake, what's all that noise!" Mrs. Finster's head stuck out of a trailer. "We're trying to take a spelling test in here!"

"I . . . I have a note for you," I called. "From Mrs. Schultz."

"Well, give it over!" She snapped. I looked at Akila, and Akila looked back at me.

"She can't," said Akila. "She'll fall through."

"Then you can deliver it to me in spring thaw," said Mrs. Finster.

That seemed a long time away. I didn't feel so afraid with a grown-up watching, especially Mrs. Finster. Even the snow wouldn't mess with Mrs. Finster. I sheepishly teetered over, sinking to my knees but no deeper, and delivered the note. She read it with a serious face.

"Mmgph!" Miss Finster made a grumpy noise. "Tell her anything but anchovies and black olives is fine," she said, before she slammed the window shut.

In fact, I should not have been afraid. The weeks of cold and the weight of the snow and traffic had packed everything below into cakes of ice, but the city had to carry on, and, slowly, brave delivery trucks began reappearing on the streets. So began a new game, especially popular with boys, called "skitching." Boys would grab on to the back fender of a delivery truck and be pulled along on the icy streets for blocks.

The vice principal came to each classroom and warned us not to do it, that it was extremely dangerous, that the drivers couldn't even see us back there and they might skid or stop suddenly. . . . Her warning was like a commercial to some of the more daring boys. But then one day, the skitching came to a sudden stop.

There were whispers on the playground.

Dead.

Dead? Who?

That boy, in 105, the other fifth-grade room.

He wore that sweater sometimes. Remember him?

Are you sure?

Yeah. Dead. His friend was with him. . . .

Dead.

Mrs. Schultz let the boy's friend come to our classroom to tell his story, and the vice principal came, too. I could tell by the way they looked at him they thought it would be good for him to talk about it and good for us to hear it, so we wouldn't make up stories or ask him all the time. Many of the boys in our class knew the boy who died. It seemed that suddenly they knew him well. They all searched hard for something they remembered, like a coin they had forgotten in a pocket but suddenly were digging deep for.

I remember he liked chocolate milk. Remember? He asked me

once, did I want mine, and I said no, you can have it.

He gave me a turn on the swings, he never hogged the swings. He was a good guy.

But truthfully, we all knew the only one who really knew him was this boy, his friend, the one who was there. He wore a ski cap over his curly hair; even the vice principal didn't make him take it off. He had a strange orange-brown complexion, freckles, and large teeth. He seemed eager to talk. We all leaned forward.

"His hand slipped and he fell. His head hit a funny way. His eyes rolled back in his head. I yelled bloody murder. Bloody murder!" His voice rose, and so did the hair on our backs. "Everyone heard me; windows opened and women started yelling for someone to call an ambulance. Even the driver heard me. The truck braked and the guy jumped out and ran over. I told him, he's dead. I knew he was, there was a trickle of blood on his ear. He picked him up, even though someone yelled, 'don't move him, don't move him!' He picked him up anyway, and we both started screaming.

The man yelled at me"—the boy glanced at the vice principal—"'Why the hell you kids got to play like that?' And I said, 'I don't know.' Then he grabbed me, too, and held me so tight, and started crying and crying, real hard."

Oh, my God, I thought. Make him stop. *Make him stop!*

But he didn't stop. "That wasn't the scariest part," he said, and waited. I looked at him and wondered, Is he enjoying this? He had a funny look on his face, but it wasn't exactly a smile. He seemed to be trying to get enough breath to say the next thing. Air seemed to be working differently for him.

"What?" One boy couldn't take it anymore.

"The worst part," he said, "was. When I went. With the policeman. To his mother. To tell what happened. And the policeman told her. 'Your son is dead.' And she was doing the dishes. And she wouldn't stop doing the dishes. So the policeman. Said it over again. And she said, 'No, not my son. There must be some mistake. He's on his way home from school.' And

I said, 'Mira, look, it's me, it's no mistake! It was him!'
And she smiled and touched my cheek and said, 'No,
no, you are mistaken. It was not my son. My son is a
little late sometimes. It was not my son.' And she kept
saying it until she was screaming it and throwing
things." He touched both his ears at the same time, as
if his ears were still ringing, and many of us touched
our ears, too. He noticed he did this and put his hands
down and laughed at himself. A quiet laugh rippled all
through the aisles. "Then the policemen held her and
then they took me away." He looked at us with old
eyes. "She's gonna wait for her son forever," he said,
"but he ain't ever coming home. So just you be
careful." He pointed at all of us. "If something happens
to you, your momma's gonna miss you."

How could he not cry? We stared at him with all
of our eyes and all of our mouths open, panting like
dogs to keep from bawling. The friend shifted on his
feet and smiled unexpectedly and humbly, like a boy
who wasn't used to doing well in school but found him-

self to be giving a good report.

"People deal with death in different ways," explained Mrs. Schultz. She extended sympathies on behalf of our class. Then she told us about a moment of silence. We had one. I didn't know the boy, so I just watched the second hand on the big classroom clock sweep carelessly over a minute that boy didn't get to live.

"Now we all know the story." The vice principal patted the friend's shoulders. "So you don't have to ask him any more about it, hm?" She straightened. "And are you ever going skitching again?" she asked her spokesperson.

"No way! No way, man," he said. "But if I do, I'll hold on real tight."

The thaw came and ran along the gutters, the last of the winter's tears. It muddied the big park and quenched the thirsty earth below. Clover came up that spring like never before, and dandelion seeds floated all around us like the ghosts of a million snowflakes.

5

Stealing the Afikomen

Let me tell you something about religion.

My parents sent me to Hebrew school at a conservative synagogue even though we weren't observant Jews. They wanted me to learn about my culture, and this synagogue was the most conveniently located. Rabbi Deitcher was our teacher. He was stout, with a short brown beard and mustache, twinkly eyes, and a chortling laugh. He was always so pleased with us for any little good thing we did. He was like Santa's Jewish younger brother. Mom warned me against sharing that observation with him, along with the fact that we put up a Christmas tree every December.

We learned to write Hebrew letters: *shin, gimmel, hey.* Soon I could sound out sentences, but I didn't know what they meant and couldn't imagine knowing. Still, it was a mysterious and musical language, and I liked to study it. If we studied hard we might someday have a *bar* or *bat mitzvah*, a party that would rival our weddings and usher us into adulthood. Rumor had it that this party also meant we would get a lot of cash gifts from our friends and neighbors, which we could put aside for college. Which friends and neighbors are going to give me these cash gifts? I wondered. The girls turning double Dutch in front of the high-rise who always mooch off my corn chips? I wasn't holding my breath.

Rabbi Deitcher tried to teach us Jewish history. He told us to put our heads down and close our eyes and then told us about how during World War II, Nazis came and burst in and separated children just like us from their parents and put them in showers that spewed poison gas instead of water. When the rabbi pounded on the door with both fists to imitate Germans breaking in, I almost jumped out of my skin.

Rabbi Deitcher told us Jews have never thrown the first punch. Never, ever, *ever*.

"Never?" I asked, just to be sure.

"*Never*," he repeated.

"Well, " I said, "sometimes I hit my brother first. And I'm Jewish."

Rabbi Deitcher chuckled, then cleared his throat. "Never unprovoked," he clarified, holding his finger in the air. "We never *start* anything."

I had something to say about that, too, but I figured it wouldn't make me look too good, so I kept my mouth shut.

Rabbi Deitcher taught us in a classroom, but one day he took us into the temple, which was all aglow in stained glass. He took the Torah from the ark to show us. It was the holy book, written on heavy scrolls and wrapped in velvet. The rabbi told us that during services the Torah is carried, and if we ever see anyone drop the Torah, we must fast for a month.

"What's 'fast'?"

"You must not eat."

Not eat! For a month! Our refrigerator at home had been broken for weeks, and there was precious little enough to eat. I certainly wasn't about to eat any less; I got hungry just thinking about it. I closed my eyes tightly as the rabbi returned the Torah to the ark. I wasn't taking any chances.

"God is in this temple," the rabbi told us, "but not only in this temple. God is everywhere. Let's name the places. At home, at school . . ."

"How about behind those curtains?" I asked.

The rabbi smiled. "Everywhere." He lectured on, but I couldn't stop staring at the heavy red drapes. Was God really *everywhere*? Even behind the drapes? What sort of God were we talking about, that hides behind drapes?

Rabbi Deitcher escorted us out, but I hung back and peeked behind the drapes. I didn't see anything, and breathed easily. God is not a creep, I decided. God is good. God has better things to do beside hiding behind curtains and spying on little girls. Maybe God has a lot of TVs and every life has a channel, I thought. I didn't know. I still don't.

* * *

One of my teachers from school, who also belonged to the congregation, kindly offered to take me to a Seder in the basement of the synagogue. The Seder is a symbolic meal eaten during Passover, a very holy time on the Jewish calendar, during which we remember that we were once slaves in Egypt. When fleeing Egypt and being pursued by a furious king, the Jews were in such a hurry that they didn't have time to wait for the bread to rise, and flat matzo crackers remind us of this. At the start of the Passover meal, an announcement came from the head table where all the rabbis sat. They said they were taking a special piece of matzo, the *afikomen*, and wrapping it in a cloth. It would be placed under the head rabbi's chair. And the boy who could take it out from under the rabbi's chair at some point in the evening without the wise old rabbi's noticing could ask for *any*thing he wanted.

ANYthing? I thought, and as if to answer me, the rabbis chorused, ANYTHING! ANYTHING in the WHOLE WIDE WORLD!

Well, this sounded like a very good prize indeed.

Here, all this time I had never been to an ocean, though I heard it was very lovely, with shells and fish and waves and such. And now, I could *have* an ocean! After all, an ocean was part of ANYthing, wasn't it? And what about stars and planets? No, no, it had to be in the whole wide world, not outside of it. What else? What else? The services began. We dipped bitter herbs in salt water to remind us of tears, and I was allowed to drink wine, though it gave me a strange, cramping stomachache. Everyone sang merrily and swayed. I could not stop thinking, though, about the afikomen under the rabbi's chair. Finally, I decided I must take it, if only to be able to pay attention to the rest of the service.

A holy prayer began. I pretended to drop my napkin and went under the table, where I crawled on my belly the long way toward the head table, to the row of black shoes that belonged to the rabbis. And under the middle seat . . .

There it was! No one had taken it yet!

The head rabbi's feet were thumping to the rhythm of the prayer. Gingerly, I reached between them and took the afikomen, then stumbled along on my elbows and knees, back to my seat. I sat back up, wiped my mouth casually with my napkin with one hand, and concealed the afikomen against my chair back. I couldn't help smiling.

Throughout the evening, I saw the heads of boys in the rows of guests disappear, and then reappear some minutes later, their mouths twisted with disappointment. I was at first very pleased with myself for acting so quickly, but then a worry made its way into my mind. Did or did not the rabbi say that the *boy* who took the afikomen could have anything? Would it matter that a girl had taken it? Were girls not supposed to want prizes? Had I behaved in an unladylike way? If it wasn't meant for a girl, was it like stealing? Would the rabbis be angry? Would I be punished? Should I put it back? I watched as another boy's head reappeared, and felt myself harden. No, I decided, I won't put it back. It wasn't fair to offer anything in the world just to boys, and I would tell them so. Better, I would show them so. I looked at the clock. I was feeling exhausted from all the worry.

Finally, when I thought the evening would never end, the last song was sung. The old rabbi stood up and the room grew quiet. "And now," he said, "I will check under my chair to see if any boy was *brave* enough, *clever* enough, to steal the afikomen." He looked under his chair. "It's gone!" he exclaimed. Everyone moaned and applauded. I felt myself start to quake.

"Now, a promise is a promise," the rabbi continued. "The brave and clever boy who has taken the afikomen can ask for ANYTHING he wants. ANYTHING! In the whole! Wide! World!"

"*Ooohhh,*" said everyone.

"What will he ask for? What wish is waiting in a little boy's heart? We will soon find out." The rabbi winked. "Will the boy who has taken the afikomen from under the rabbi who has seen a hundred Passovers *please rise!*"

Everyone murmured and looked around, leaning over the tables to see which boy was standing.

No boy was standing.

Nobody was standing at all.

Ooohhh, I thought. *This is bad.* I wished my mother and father were there. They would know what to do. But I was all alone.

"What's this?" said the rabbi. "Surely one of you has taken it. It's not there. Matzos don't grow legs and walk away by themselves, do they?" Everyone laughed. "So, come. Don't be shy. Stand and collect whatever it is you want in the whole world."

Well, we can't just sit here all night, I decided. I swallowed hard and stood up. I reached behind me and took out the afikomen and held it in the air.

A small gasp rose.

I swallowed again. "I took it," I announced, in case anybody didn't notice. "But I'm not a boy," I also announced, in case anybody didn't notice.

At this, the rabbis at the head table at once gathered themselves into a feverish huddle, like blackbirds around freshly laid seed. "One moment while we consider the situation," a voice called. People murmured, and the boys who had earlier hunted for the treasure snickered at me. Little girls looked at me wide-eyed. They must be shocked, I thought. Or did they look . . . excited?

The rabbis' huddle opened up and they faced us. "We have come to a decision," a younger rabbi said. "We have decided: a child is a child. Whoever has the *chutzpah*, boy or girl, to take the afikomen from under the chair of the head rabbi deserves the prize."

A cheer went up. Everyone applauded again. "My student! My student!" Rabbi Deitcher called from the end of the table. I felt myself breathe again.

"So let's get down to business, Esmé," said the head rabbi. "ANYthing you want. ANYthing in the whole wide world. . . ."

Yes, yes, I know, I thought, my mind racing. I had already had one wish granted, to steal the afikokmen, and a second wish in not getting in trouble for it. So now I had to think quickly of a greedy third wish, which I had not seriously considered. ANYthing? Now that my mind was cleared of trouble, the answer came quickly.

"Rabbi, if I may have anything in the world, I would like the kitchen of the synagogue."

He looked at me quizzically. "Excuse me," he said. "I am old. My hearing must be playing tricks on me."

"The . . . the kitchen," I repeated. "Just during the day. And of course, I won't use it on Saturdays." People looked at me as though they were having trouble with their hearing. "It has a working oven, doesn't it? And a refrigerator?" My mother and father would be so pleased. Cold butter and milk again!

"Yes, but . . . but what does a young girl want with a kitchen of a synagogue?"

"I would like to run a bakery through the kitchen," I explained. "I would like to make cookies with pink sugar dots and birthday cakes with roses . . . and trains." I threw in generously to the dumbfounded boys. I felt myself growing more and more excited. "I will be happy to make cakes and cookies for anyone here who needs them."

"It's a good idea!" Rabbi Deitcher shook his finger in the air. "My student!"

"Yes, it is very kind," agreed the head rabbi, "and very enterprising. But we cannot give you the kitchen of the synagogue. Would you not rather have a nice doll?"

"Thank you," I said as politely as I could, "but I would not. I thought the prize was anything in the whole wide world. I am not asking for the entire synagogue. I am asking only to use the kitchen."

The rabbis gave me a worried look and resumed their huddle. I heard people around me starting to argue.

"So who is using it? Let her use it!"

"She should bake in her mother's kitchen if she wants to bake."

"The rabbi did say *anything*."

"*Anything* is a figure of speech."

"The rabbi said she could ask for anything in the world, not get it. Ask! Not get!"

"What are you, a flimflammer? Of course getting is what the rabbi meant."

"Would we get a discount on mandel bread?" some-one joked.

Finally, the rabbis turned around. "We have come to a decision. The head rabbi himself will select a special surprise and it will be presented to Esmé in Hebrew school!"

The thought of more waiting was too excruciating to imagine, but it was clear that they were not going to give me the kitchen.

"Okay," I said. "Thank you."

Cheers and applause thundered.

Finally, Tuesday afternoon arrived and I waited as Rabbi Deitcher went into the back room to get my prize. My classmates seemed as eager as I was. Maybe it's a cake, I hoped. A chocolate cake with whipped-cream flowers and a doll with eyes that opened and closed on a heart-shaped stand. Five months before my birthday! And everyone would enjoy it.

The rabbi brought out a little box tied with metallic

cord, a box much too small to hold a cake. I opened the box and pulled out a gold necklace with a little gold charm, a *chai*, the symbol of living. I was instantly offended. I tried to hide my disappointment with every molecule in my body. *Don't be spoiled*, I scolded myself. *You ought to be ashamed! A real gold necklace! Won't that look pretty with your dresses!* But another, louder part of me thought, *What the heck kind of girl does that rabbi think I am?* Then I realized: he thinks I'm like every girl. He thinks I want gold and jewelry instead of cake and cookies. Instead of tools and bread. *Don't be angry*, I told myself. *It takes more than stealing a single matzo to prove I am not this kind of girl. It's going to take a lot of time. Maybe a lifetime.* I grew clammy at the thought of this chore. Rabbi Deitcher passed out jelly candies to celebrate, which made me feel a little better.

When I came home, I gave the *chai* to my mother. Then I told her I didn't want to go to Hebrew school anymore.

"Why not?" she asked.

"It's too much about getting stuff," I said. "I don't want to care so much about getting stuff."

My father overheard, and went in the other room where he gathered some books in a pile and handed them to me. I looked at the spines. *Zen Flesh, Zen Bones. The Secret of the Golden Flower. Siddhartha.* A pile of books about Buddhism.

"Mazel tov," he said.

6

Love Has No Experts

Let me tell you something about love.

Wait, wait! Don't close the book. Books are one of the best places to learn about love, though there certainly are other sources for information. If you want to know the first initial of the person you are going to marry, there are many ways to do it. You can skip a rope while you recite the alphabet, until you miss. You can twist the stem of an apple while you recite the alphabet, until the stem comes out. You can write out the alphabet and think how many children you would like to have, and then cross out a letter every time you arrive at that number until you have only one letter left. But really, why do you want to go to all this trouble to know the first initial of your future bride or groom? The information is quite useless. What is less useless is the promise that somebody out there will love you, for better or worse (hopefully, better), in sickness and in health (hopefully, health), and richer or poorer (so buy lottery tickets).

This is what I knew about love when I was your age.

Love Is Mysterious

I was very excited when Gypsies moved onto our block because I heard they could tell fortunes, and so they might be able to tell me more than a twisted apple stem could. It turned out they weren't really the store-front fortune-telling kind of Gypsies, although they were very superstitious and wore lots of protective amulets. There were more people living in their apartment than I could keep track of. Some of them were monstrous looking, brutish and pale and beady-eyed, and others looked like fairy-tale heroes, olive-skinned and gleaming, as beautiful as any people I have ever seen. They all spoke to each other in a language called Romany. There was a tent pitched inside the apartment and not much furniture otherwise. Even though they didn't seem to have much stuff, they were always having yard sales, selling things like hangers, yellowing porcelain plates, bent forks wrapped in bundles, and combination locks that they did not know the combinations to. Just a dollar each!

My brother liked to go over to their place, and the kids would always cheer to see him at the door, especially because some of them didn't go to school at all and they were tired of one another's company. My brother liked them because they were kind of wild. They liked to play a version of tag, where someone with a stick full of crooked nails would chase the others around. They also had a seemingly endless supply of bikes.

I was less excited about visiting, because the teenage sisters with long, slender faces and buck teeth would glom on to me and talk about their dowries, and curse their parents for not being better planners. I asked them what a dowry was, and they said it was a price that the family paid to get a man to marry their daughter. I thought that sounded against the law, and told them so, but they just laughed and said, no, it wasn't against Romany law. One of the sisters offered to read tea leaves for me to see who I would marry. This was the offer I had been waiting for! She put some black leaves in a cup of steaming water and swirled them around before draining it. "Someone in hotel management," she said, and passed the cup along to the other women in the room, including her mother, who all peered in and gave short, matter-of-fact nods. I looked into the cup and saw a mulchy-looking pile at the bottom of the cup, and could not for the life of me figure out how they saw the future in it.

"Now do you," I said.

She repeated the procedure, looked, and burst into tears, running out of the room and slamming a door somewhere down the hall.

The women passed the cup again and nodded before exiting to console her. Her mother took a quick glance and rolled her eyes. "Fast food, same as always."

The Gypsies weren't the only family with superstitious women. My grandmother told me a story that when she was a young woman she went to a party and there was a Ouija board, which is a magical instrument. You lay your fingers on a tiny table with a window in it. The table moves seemingly by some invisible hand over letters of the alphabet on a board, spelling out your heart's desire or answer to any question. My grandmother asked what the name of her husband would be, and the board spelled out R-I-C-H-A-R-D. And lo and behold! Who should she marry but a man named Richard?

"That's amazing, that story about Grandma and the Ouija board spelling out your name," I remarked to my grandfather in a private moment.

He beckoned me closer with his finger. "My name is Isidore," he said.

LOVE IS ENTERTAINING

My parents seemed to think that the television was not

94

only educational but the greatest invention since the wheel, and we were encouraged to watch as much as possible. "We live in a time of such great entertainment!" my father would testify and my mother would nod and sigh and all but get up and smooch the set. The old Zenith had a channel-changing screwdriver shoved into the hole that used to house the dial, and its antenna had been broken some time ago, but was amended with a wire coat hanger wrapped in aluminum foil. It was on fairly constantly, and its drone became like the voice of another family member.

Since I watched between three and seven hours of television a day, the lines between real life and what happened on the screen were a little smudged at times. I had more crushes on cartoon characters than I had on real boys. The Japanese race car driver Speed Racer was the most heartbreakingly handsome cartoon man. The mysterious Racer X competed against Speed, hiding his secret identity as Speed's older brother. Speed, unfortunately for me, was already attached to a gorgeous girlfriend named Trixie. She had short hair held in place by a little barrette, and long legs that buckled at the knees. I wanted to be exactly like her and then steal Speed from her. I practiced saying "Speed! *Speed!*" in that breathy, desperate way she had, and then chuckled a little to myself at the thought of Trixie gasping as I walked away with Speed on my arm. Everyone on that show was always gasping, every turn of plot or road was so harrowing. I thought it was also very exciting that Speed knew how to drive and had his own car, which he even named the *Mach 5*. Who names a car? Cool people, that's who. Cool Japanese cartoon people.

I also had a thing for a character named Woody Woodpecker, which was embarrassing, not only because he was a cartoon but because he was a bird, and not only because he was a bird but because he was a horribly *obnoxious* bird who would actually peck other cartoon characters on the head. But he had an infectious laugh, and sometimes called people "Daddy-o," which made me melt a little bit inside. That was the first time I understood that if a guy can make a girl smile, it really doesn't matter so much what he looks like.

There was one cartoon I watched the most, called "Popeye the Sailor Man." It was about a pipe-smoking sailor who was kind of deformed and had a speech impediment, but when he ate spinach, he suddenly became very good at punching people. He was in love with Olive Oyl, who was no great beauty and a little whiny and seemed to own only one outfit, but managed to have a lot of admirers. She had some sort of relationship with an abusive, hulking boyfriend named Bluto. She used the attraction Popeye and Bluto felt for her to create a rivalry between them.

I always thought Olive had a lot of confidence, because if I had only one dress and no shape like she did, I wouldn't be so quick to play head games with the guys I liked. I paid a lot of attention to Popeye and tried to learn from it, because it seemed very realistic. I mean, you couldn't make people like that up, could you?

When I was home from school one day, they showed *Wuthering Heights* on the Channel 9 *Morning Movie*. In the movie, the grown-ups were hysterical with grief because they didn't have enough time to spend together. When they were finally in the same room, the man yelled in the woman's face about how much he loved her, and the woman seemed to be half fainted because of the yelling. They were very concerned about dying and not being able to haunt each other, so I was very patient and waited about two hours for some ghosts to appear, but they never did. All in all it was a pretty mushy show, but the one awesome part was that the woman called her boyfriend's name, "Heathcliff! Heathcliff!" And it could be heard from miles away, not even using a telephone.

I would lie in bed at night, thinking about how improbable this was. It would drive me crazy. How could she say "Heathcliff" from way across the moor and he could hear it? Come on! It was impossible! I didn't know much about science—cell phones hadn't even been invented yet—but I did know that when you talk to someone far away, there's usually some kind of wiring involved. Then again, I had heard of the "power of love," so maybe if you said something really affectionate it would create a kind of electrical force that could actually carry through the atmosphere.

I knew from watching Mickey Rooney in *Young Tom Edison* on the Channel 9 *Morning Movie* that when there is a scientific question, the only way to find the answer is by testing and observation. So I decided to test my hypothesis. Eric Fostnot was a new boy who had just transferred into my class. He was taller than the other boys and tripped over things when he walked. He had brown hair that was so long and soft that he had to keep tossing it out of his brown eyes, and sometimes when he was working he would blow his bangs out of the way. He was so handsome that I thought if he were crossing the street and a car was coming and he was about to be struck, I just might have to throw myself in front of it to push him out of the way, and when he would lift my battered body in his arms he would say, *Oh, Esmé, my brave, brave Esmé, how could you do that for me?* and the heavens would grant me just enough breath to reply, *Don't mention it, Eric, it's not that big a deal,* and through his tears he would choke, *But I love you, Esmé, my darling! Haunt me! Be with me always! Take any form! Drive me mad!* But could I hear him? No. It would be too late. My life would have already been sacrificed, a pittance to pay to preserve this angel on earth. Just as a matter of science, I mention it.

I went out on my front porch after my parents were asleep. I licked my finger and raised it in the air to determine the direction of the wind. I closed my eyes and mustered all the love power I possibly could and waited for a good strong breeze before whispering, "I love you, Eric Fostnot!"

Had it worked? Had I said it loudly enough? Had I said it in the right direction? Surely, it must have reached him—he *couldn't* live that far away—we went to the same school, after all. I tried again. "I love you, Eric Fostnot!" I cried out more bravely. "From Esmé!" I added, for good measure, and then waited another eternity. Wait, what was that? Was that *My darling! Be with me always—take any form—drive me mad*? No, it was a cat jumping on a trash lid. It was a front door opening and closing. It was the hum of the news in a neighbor's apartment. I waited on the porch for about forty-five minutes, shivering in my pajamas, with my arms crossed, and received no reply. What a cruel boy! I thought. What a cruel, inconsiderate boy!

When I went to school the next day, Eric Fostnot went about his business, tripping over things and blowing his hair as if nothing had happened. Every small movement seemed heartless and cold. He didn't even look at me! Not that he had ever looked at me, but now, it was so clearly deliberate. After all that had passed between us! By the end of the day I was so mad at Eric that I couldn't stand the sight of him. He had absolutely wuthered my heights.

The next night, I went on the porch. "Eric Fostnot,

you stinkball! I hope you're happy!"

I was glad when he transferred out.

Love Is Confusing

I had a classmate, a pretty blond girl named Kirsten, from Germany, with a perky doll-like nose, and eyes as clear and blue and charming as a fishbowl on a windowsill. I knew she was from Germany because she said she was from Germany; she was always talking about how she was from Germany. Every day, she worked it into the conversation somehow, and I mean, she really worked it. When they served hot dogs for lunch, she would ask the lunch lady, "Are these frankfurters imported from Germany? Because I'm from Germany!" or "Mrs. Schultz! What kind of dog is in the story we are reading? I was just wondering if it was a German shepherd. Because, you know what? I'm from Germany!" Whenever the gym teacher made us line up by height we'd end up beside each other. I asked her what she remembered about Germany, and she said nothing, she came here when she was three months old. I told her that it seemed she had been here long enough to call herself American if she wanted to, but she said, "No, thank you, I prefer to consider myself European. Being from Germany, you know." I said, okay, fine.

Not only did Kirsten know a lot about Germany, she also claimed to be Wise to the Ways of Men, especially men in the fifth grade. She announced on the playground to all of us girls that for the nominal fee of fifty cents, she would offer lessons. Fifty cents could buy coconut snowballs, or a big bag of Jay's sour cream-and-onion potato chips, or five—count 'em—*five* packs of Now and Laters, which were thick squares of fruit-flavored taffy that left fluorescent sugar rims around your gum line. But I gave her the money, because knowledge is power.

When she came over to my front stoop after school, she said first things first—she had to know who I liked. When I told her his name was None of Your Business, she clucked her tongue and said, real exasperated-like, that she could not *possibly* be expected to help me if she didn't know who I liked, because she couldn't *tailor* her *instruction* to meet my needs. I had no idea what she was talking about, but it sounded very professional, so I told her that I guessed José was the nicest boy in class. I warmed pleasantly at the thought of him; how he sent me a marble wrapped in a crumpled piece of paper from across the room, how he asked me to dance at the class Christmas party, how he told me when I grew up I would have nice legs.

"José!" Kirsten's lip curled and she stuck out her tongue in a gagging way, her shoulders contorted, her outstretched fingers formed a frozen frame around her face, and her nostrils flared. It was an expression a little bit like a blond version of the monsters carved into the totem poles I had seen at the Field Museum of Natural History. "*Ewg!* Well, *okay! Anyway!*" It took her a moment to compose herself. "The secret to getting a man is"—drumroll, please, as she leaned in close and whispered in my ear—"butt-switching."

"Butt-switching?" *Butt*-switching? I already wanted my fifty cents back.

"Like this. Watch," she commanded. She walked down the stairs, paused, took a deep breath, and then walked down the sidewalk. "See?"

"See what?"

She sucked in another breath and tried again. I also tried again, concentrating very hard on the seat of her pants. Her gait was somewhat like a duck, tail feathers pointing north, then south with every alternating step. "Now, you try it." She changed places with me, held her chin in her hand, leaned forward, ready to critique my southern hemisphere. I walked back and forth across the sidewalk. "More sway! More sway!" She directed.

Sway what?

She sighed. I sighed. I was obviously hopeless, and returned to the stoop. "It takes practice," she offered. "Two hours a day, you'll have it down in a week."

"Huh," I said. "Got anything else?"

"Well, there's this," she said, sucking in her cheeks.

"What?" I asked. She pointed urgently at her sucked-in cheeks. So I sucked in my cheeks as well.

"Yeah," she tooted through her little pinpoint lips, because she was still sucking. "Men love this." They *do*? I wondered. Men seemed crazier by the minute.

She took out her Bonne Bell strawberry lip gloss and reapplied. "And when men are talking to you? Laugh. Laugh a lot. Like this: 'ha-ha-ha-ha-ha!'" She reared her head back and let it rip. "Ahhhh," she sighed. "That's so *funny*."

"What's so funny?"

"The joke a boy just told."

"What was the joke?" I liked jokes.

"It doesn't matter what the joke was! Hel*l*o!" I think Kirsten was the originator of using "hello" as an insult instead of a greeting. She made her eyes big at me and my ignorance. Still, she looked very pretty and silly when she did that, so I laughed my real laugh.

"Not bad. And if all else fails, there is a magic song." Kirsten half whispered, looking side to side before deciding to disclose this final pearl of wisdom. "If you put it on the record player, men cannot resist you. It's called 'The Way We Were.'"

"I don't think I have that record," I said.

"Then you can sing it. 'Meeeeemmmmmm'ries, light the cuh-cuh-corners of mah miiiiiind.'" She had the strangest voice, all breathy and whispery and stuttering on purpose. She closed her eyes when she sang, and when she was finished, Kirsten leaned in confidentially. "Whenever my big sister puts it on, she and her boyfriend make out for hooooours. I'm telling you. It's *magical* when Barbra Streisand sings that song."

"You like Barbra Streisand?"

"Of course! She's the greatest singer in the history of the world! Why? Don't you like her?"

"Sure," I said. "She's great. I mean, I'm just kind of surprised. . . . I guess I didn't realize Barbra Streisand was big in Germany."

"Of course she's big in Germany." She lifted her chin. "Germans have *impeccable* taste." She closed her eyes again and sang. "People. People who need people. Are the looooooooooockiest peeeeeeeple!" When she opened her eyes, they were shining, and our lesson was concluded.

"Well, thanks, Kirsten."

"You're welcome," She waved a stiff-handed good-bye like Miss America, excuse me, Miss Germany, walking down the street using her come-hither waddle that turned not only the heads of men, but of everyone coming home from work and toddlers in their strollers.

I watched her all the way down the block.

Within a week, I spied Kirsten leaning against the chain-link fence with José, offering him a Now and Later from one of her many packs. As she moved in closer to him, she sucked in her cheeks, bent her head my way, and flashed me a wicked look. Even though I felt as if I had been struck, I did not crumple to the ground. I was bolted in place by my own jealousy. But of whom? Of what? She was evil, yes, but beautiful. I wanted what she had more than I wanted him.

I looked at Kirsten, her steely eyes and her blond hair floating around her head in a false halo. Confusion filled me like a fog, but on a clearer day I would see forever: José was one lucky guy.

Love Is Loud

My parents didn't get along all the time. One would say something, and the other would say something louder, and then the other would say something louder still, like they were in a steady race to the top of a staircase where every stair was an increase in volume. But then my mom would do something tricky, like all of a sudden say something that was five stairs down, and that would make my father shout something from the very tip-top of the staircase. This terrible tuneless opera would eventually drive me all the way down my own real staircase to sit on the stoop of my building, where I could hear them arguing from the street. There were usually other kids sitting on the stoop, who were generally polite enough not to mention anything about it other than something conversational, like, "My parents fought last Tuesday," which they probably did. You could pretty much go to anyone's apartment and watch the show there if you lost interest in what was going on at your own place. The reason everyone was arguing was because everyone on my block was broke, and money is a big reason grown-ups fight. It is really a hopeless fight, because I still have never met anyone who was paid for arguing with their husband or wife, no matter how well they do it. It doesn't stop them from practicing, though, just in case.

I knew the coast was clear when my father played "Wild World" by Cat Stevens on the record player. It wasn't a signal, just something he happened to play whenever my mother made him angry. He would pace back and forth in front of the speakers, nodding in agreement every now and then, while my mother sat frowning in the kitchen, smoking her cigarettes.

I would say something to cheer my mother up, like, "Daddy is like a barking dog when he gets mad, isn't he?" but it wouldn't work. My mother's face would turn white and she'd say, "Don't talk about your father that way. Your father is a genius." Then she would crush her cigarette on a plate and swirl the ash around in thoughtless circles, the corners of her mouth turned down. "You know, there was a study." She would brighten, or try to. "Kids whose parents fight grow up to be great writers."

I smiled to be polite, but inside I thought, well, then, I guess I'm living on a block with a whole bunch of Shakespeares.

I thought something else inside, too—a secret, a wish that I was ashamed of. *I hope they get a divorce*, I would wish. Yes, I would actually wish it. Then I would scramble to get hold of that wish, as if it were a delicate vase that I almost dropped, scramble to put it back on its shelf. *No, of course not, I don't want everything to be in a million pieces, a million shards that can't even be swept up in the dustpan. I don't want everything to disintegrate into sharp particles that will cut at the bottom of the feet of everyone who lives in this house with every step we take.* Of course, I didn't wish that, or not exactly that. I just wished that the needle of the record player would never drop again on "Wild World." But part of love is a record playing, a needle that drops over and over, repeat, repeat, until the voices are scratched and the song is tired. But that's all right, all the scratches and skips, the knowing what line comes next. Sometimes a song just gets you. You know?

7

Grandma's Fun House

Let me tell you about grandparents.

There was a time I had all four grandparents alive at once, and two of my great-grandparents. One was more fabulous than the next. They were all divorced from each other and loved adventure and eating at nice restaurants.

My great-grandparents came from Russia. Nanny spoke Yiddish, which sounded like scolding, so I was scared of her; but she would coax me out with ridiculous amounts of candy bars that filled the produce drawer in her refrigerator. Papa was smaller and gentler and looked Chinese. He ran a barbershop from his basement and played violin for his customers.

My Grandma Raisy was a worldly and glamorous brunette who never seemed to grow old. She brought us a roasted chicken every Wednesday and would take my brother and me to see any movie we wanted to see.

Sometimes she went to places like China and Italy, and brought me back exotic pens and lipstick holders.

My Grandpa Sy was so handsome that he matched Grandma Raisy, but he was a gambler when he was young and caused a lot of heartache that way. But when he was older, he lived in Florida and ran the most beautiful delicatessen I ever saw, where he would make sandwiches too big to get your mouth around. He used to work in Hollywood and liked to yell at my dad for not taking me to auditions. When he sang, it sounded like he was talking instead of singing, like his favorite vocalist, Al Jolson. Sy told jokes that made you laugh until you thought you couldn't breathe, and had a rule that he would never take a normal picture. The photo albums were full of him looking like he was making a great speech or being murdered.

My Grandpa Isidore was a great romantic who loved to quote Shakespeare and grew huge peonies in his backyard. He was debonair on the tennis courts and at the swimming pool, and loved to take ladies ballroom dancing. His favorite expression seemed to be, "You don't know what you're missing, little darling." He was very generous and bought all the women in my family expensive jewelry they always treasured. He wrote poetry that the family treasured at least as much.

But the Grandma that I knew the most growing up was my mother's mother, Grandma Evelyn, just called Grandma.

Grandma lived on the other side of the block from us. We could see her back porch from our back porch. She lived in an apartment that was once one huge apartment, but was split in two to accommodate more renters. You had to unlock a door which opened into an empty parlor, then go down a long, dark hall, turn on a light (hurry!) and unlock another door to get into her apartment. If you wanted her to buzz you in, you had to make sure to ring the bell three times, and then all the locks would open for you.

Grandma had a lot of interesting things.

Grandma had rotary phones. That meant you had to

stick your finger in a little hole in a wheel over a number and pull the wheel over to a little metal stopping point, and then take your finger out and let it spin back, *click-click-click-click-click*. You had to do this with every number and it was easy to mess up, so it took a long time to dial, compared to modern telephones. It was kind of fun, but I always worried what would happen if Grandma had an emergency.

Nine.

click-click-click-click-click-click-click-click-click

One.

click

One.

click

Emergencies would just have to wait.

Grandma's kitchen/dining room was where most of the action took place. It had a big pantry. In it was an old icebox with a metal freezer that would frost over into a big white marshmallowy bulge with only a little sunken belly button to shove the ice tray into. In the pantry was also Grandma's overflowing collection of tiny little boxes of jellies and packets of ketchup from restaurants. If there were ever a war, she would have more rations of single-serving condiments than anyone. Grandma had pretty crystal serving pieces all piled up on the pantry shelves. She had an endless supply of almond windmill cookies. Sometimes they were fresh and sometimes they seemed to be made out of a real windmill. If she offered them to you, you had to take your chances. Grandma had neatly typed poems on yellowing paper taped up all around her kitchen sink. Many of the poems my grandma had written herself. She was a very good writer and sometimes had them published in the newspaper, or won contests, which was exciting. She always had a cheerful dish towel hanging nearby. On her kitchen table was a shiny little toaster oven, where she might make you a "pig in a poke," which was a hot dog stuffed with melted American cheese and wrapped in bacon.

Grandma had an upright piano in her living room and lots of old sheet music. She would take out a brittle copy of *Victor Herbert's Piano Album for the Young* and play haltingly while I sang:

> *Bob-by Shaf-to's gone to sea,*
> *Silver buckles on his knee,*
> *He'll come back and marry me,*
> *Pret-ty Bob-by Shaf-to.*

I winced. Obviously Victor Herbert was a relative of my piano-lesson nemesis, John Schaum. Still, I liked singing and being silly in my grandma's living room. It was always clean and vacuumed, with a gold lamé couch on one side of the room and a black vinyl couch on the other. There was plenty of space behind both of them for hiding and jumping out to surprise people (if the hiding place of choice, the laundry hamper, was full). Grandma decorated in an eclectic way, which means she used more than one style. Since my grandma liked things from Asia (or "the Orient" as she put it), there was a big plastic bamboo tree and a vase of tall cattails in the living room, along with a geisha doll and a miraculous little cork sculpture of a bridge over a Japanese garden. She had an imposing painting hung above the piano. I could never quite tell what it was. For many years I thought it was a portrait of a monster's face, and I thought my grandma was very exciting to showcase such a macabre painting in the middle of her living room. As I grew older, though, I realized it was not a monster's face, but a colonial hearth with a cozy fire and two plates hung over it. This was disappointing, but the painting was so dark that it looked more like a fiery furnace, so it was still pretty good. My favorite item was a porcelain figure of Tevye, the milkman from *Fiddler on the Roof*. If you turned the figure on its stand, a little music box inside would start to play "Sunrise, Sunset." I always loved that figure and would tell her so, and she would tell me I could have it when she died. She was very excited about dying because she had bought plots in the Graceland Cemetery, where the department store mogul Marshall Field was buried. I asked her if we would all be buried there, and she shrugged. She'd only bought a few plots. "First come, first served," she said.

The door of Grandma's bathroom wouldn't close all the way, which was sometimes embarrassing. She usually had her nylon stockings soaking in the sink; the flesh-colored tangle of bloated tubes looked like a brain. Her bathtub didn't have a shower, but it did have feet like a lion. There was a table with a lot of books in the kitchen so you could grab one en route to the bathroom, which I thought was very civil. She had lots of appealing books: adventure novels by Pearl Buck set in "the Orient," collections of short stories by Dorothy Parker, volumes of advice columns by Ann Landers, and lots of books about etiquette and entertaining. I would lose track of time in there, planning imaginary parties.

Grandma's bedroom had a strange little sink offset in the wall with a porcelain bowl and brown stripes of rust running down from the hardware. Every now and then a startling sound would come up from the plumbing, like an old person trying to clear his throat from a hundred years of phlegm. If you turned the faucet handle and left it for a few minutes, it would choke up a blob of brown water. We didn't turn the faucet handle very often. It was more decorative than useful, I guess you could say. Also in Grandma's bedroom was a radiator with a little tin flap on the side so you could reach in and adjust the heat, but it also made for a very neat and secret mailbox. My redheaded cousin, Peter, who was close to my age, often spent the night at Grandma's and would leave me notes there, and when I would visit, I would find them and reply.

On my grandma's bureau next to her bed was a glass paperweight with a picture of me from a photo booth encased inside. That is how I knew my Grandma loved me. That and the way she would smooth my fingernails every time she held my hand.

Grandma had weird things to play with when we came to her house. She had metal roller skates that were missing a key and never fit right, but you could try going up and down the hall with them anyway until she screamed at you to stop. In one closet, she had a real electric train that would sometimes spark when you plugged it in and if you played with it a while it smelled like something was on fire. Grandma had a drawer full of children's books, and she was never too tired to read us our favorite, *Miss Suzy* by Miriam Young. It was about a squirrel who is bullied out of her home by some bad squirrels and goes to live in a dollhouse, where she meets some toy soldiers, who love her and avenge her mistreatment. *Miss Suzy* was always a thrill.

Grandma was always a good sport at games. She had a board game called "Your America" that she'd always offer to play with us but we would refuse because it looked too corny, so instead we would play a card game called "Kan-U-Go." Or, if it was summertime, we could sit in lawn chairs on her back porch and she would singsong, "I spy, with my little eye, something that begins with . . ." and we'd have to guess what she was looking at, with the first letter as our only clue. It was a trying game because there wasn't much to choose from:

windows of the low-rent high-rise, or the cars in the parking lot of the low-rent high-rise, or passing planes or the tops of trees, or each other's clothes. Sometimes a dragonfly would be camouflaged somewhere, or a cloud would look like something else. It was a good lesson in looking closely.

The most fun at Grandma's was going through her dresser drawers. Grandma kept every greeting card that was given to her, and it seemed like she kept every salvageable piece of wrapping paper, too. They were so pretty, I liked to spread them out and pretend I ran a stationery store.

But the best drawer was Grandma's party drawer.

Grandma threw a lot of parties, but she only entertained her own immediate family. Grandma threw birthday parties for each of her four children, even though they were grown, and sometimes she also made parties for special holidays. This was brave because my mother's side of the family was notoriously short-tempered. A facial expression or loose word could ignite

Mount Vesuvius, and usually did. Someone would march out, shouting about "you people!" or sometimes Grandma herself would get fed up and tell everyone to get out. But she never gave up. A few months would pass and the party drawer would open again, as she gambled on the hope that our family would have a few harmonious hours in succession, which sometimes happened, especially if our mouths were full of either food or song.

Since Grandma threw a lot of parties and watched her grandchildren and also worked full-time as a secretary in a hospital, she was sometimes tired. And so, one afternoon while my cousin Peter and I were visiting, she fell asleep on the black vinyl couch.

"What should we do?" asked Peter.

"I know," I said. "Grandma's always throwing parties for us. Let's throw a surprise party for her!"

This seemed like the greatest idea we had ever had, so we opened up the party drawer and laid everything out. What a stash! There were miles of streamers and crepe paper bells, frilly fruit and nut baskets and rosettes made from tissue, blowers, balloons, banners that said everything from OVER THE HILL to JUST MARRIED, plastic utensils of every color, napkins with pictures of towering pink cakes on them, and a matching tablecloth. And then there was the mother lode: packages of precious little hard-candy alphabets that Grandma used to spell out personal messages on cakes.

We had to work quickly and quietly. Who knew when Grandma would wake up? Working together, we unrolled every reel of streamer down to its tight little core and twirled and taped it to every corner of the room. Then we hung every sign, and every bell and every rosette. We blew up balloons until our heads spun.

While Peter set the table, I thought it would be a nice touch to take down every piece of crystal from the pantry and put them out. It was a party, after all! Then Peter and I filled the nut baskets with Grandma's condiment collection. We laid out the windmill cookies and every cracker we could find (Grandma also had a good restaurant cracker-packet collection) and I boiled all the hot dogs in the refrigerator. We made a fluffy punch just like Grandma taught us, using rainbow sherbet and ginger ale, in her crystal punch bowl. We hung all twelve cups around the edge with their little hooks.

Then we fell breathless into the kitchen chairs.

"We forgot something," Peter said.

"It just feels that way," I said.

"No," Peter insisted, and held up the sugar-candy letters.

We had watched Grandma and the letters during party preparations before. When Grandma took out the letters, it was always very special. She wore a serious expression as she laid them out, because she was never sure if she had all the letters she needed. She did not like us to eat the letters she wasn't using because she might need them next time. But here we were, with the whole bag of sugar letters, vowels *and* consonants, and even a couple of coveted exclamation points.

"P is for Peter," said Peter. "I call P."

"If you eat the P," I warned, "you might be an 'eter' for your birthday."

"Exactly what I want to be." Peter grinned.

"Maybe you should eat the R," I suggested. "Then at least Grandma can spell 'Pete.' Maybe she won't notice."

"But she needs the R for 'birthday.'"

"Well, she needs two P's for 'happy,'" I pointed out.

"E's are no good," said Peter. "We both need E's."

"There's vowels in every word." I tried to be smart.

"The vowels taste better," he said.

"No, they don't," I said, but his saying it already made it true. Peter was already crunching one. "What letter did you take?"

"An exclamation point."

"Are you crazy?" I took the bag from him, reached in and stuck one in my mouth.

"Which one did *you* take?"

"I don't know, I didn't look." It didn't taste like an exclamation point. It tasted like chalk, and I nearly cracked a tooth on it.

"We don't have a cake," Peter worried.

"Let's spread cream cheese on crackers," I suggested. We made a line of Saltines and started spelling. "How about, 'Happy Everything, Grandma.'"

Peter fished for letters. "Did you eat the G?"

"I don't know." G is for guilty.

"Well, then, 'Happy Everything, Evelyn.'"

"We never call her Evelyn," I said. "Besides, we don't have enough Y's."

"Here's the G," said Peter. I sighed with relief. Maybe I had eaten a Q. "But I think 'Everything' is too long."

We settled on "Hi Gran From Us."

We were exhausted, but we could not stop rotating, admiring our work.

"Let's wake her up," said Peter.

We were a little afraid, tiptoeing over. Sometimes grown-ups are in a bad mood when they wake up. But we were excited and that made us brave. Was that how Grandma felt sometimes, before a party? "Grandma! Wake up!" we hissed. She barely stirred. "We did sommmmmeethiiiiiing," we whispered cagily.

Her eyes flew open. "What did you do?"

"We made a surpriiiiiiisssse."

She sat right up. "What *kind* of surprise?"

"Come with us," we said, each taking one of her hands. We led her to the kitchen, where every single surface was covered with party.

"Oh, my God," she said. Her lower jaw unhinged.

"We used your whole party drawer, Grandma! We didn't waste," Peter announced proudly.

"Happy Everything," I cheered.

"Oh, my God," Grandma repeated. "My God!" Peter and I looked at each other. She was *happy*, right? "I feel like . . . I'm in a daze. A *dream*," she answered. She sat down, and we served punch using the ladle. She ate a cracker with grape jelly, steadily eyeing her kitchen's makeover, as we had done.

"Aren't you going to eat the candy letters, Grandma?" asked Peter.

"Those are only for decoration," said Grandma,

surprised that we didn't know. "Some of them are still good, but some got mixed in with ones from my mother that are at least twenty years old." Peter and I looked at each other again, but Grandma didn't seem to notice. "Where did you ever find so much tape?"

"The wrapping-paper drawer," I said.

"You need more tape," Peter informed her. "You're out."

"My God."

"Grandma's in shock!" Peter was bouncing up and down.

"You like it?" I asked hopefully.

"It's like a dream," Grandma repeated. "I closed my eyes and when I opened them I was in a dream." She finished off her punch. "And now I'm going to lie down on my couch and close my eyes again and when I open them I will be awake, and my whole kitchen will be just as it was, with every single thing put back exactly where it was, and I will always remember this wonderful dream where there was a beautiful party given by my grandchildren and I didn't have to clean up after it." Peter and I opened our mouths to protest, but she was already floating down the hall. "Beauuuu-tiful dreeeaamer! La-da-de-daaaa . . ."

It seemed to take twice as long to peel off all the tape, roll up all the streamers and balance the crystal back in the pantry. Peter and I could barely move by the time my mom rang the doorbell three times, at which point Grandma conveniently woke up. When they entered the kitchen, Grandma looked pleased and calm, but Mom noticed our pale faces. "Did you have fun?" Mom asked us, but Grandma answered.

"I had a lovely afternoon. I took a nice long nap and I had the most beautiful dream!"

"I hope you were good while Grandma rested."

"Oh, yes." Grandma put her arm around each of us and kissed the tops of our heads. "They were very, very good."

One morning I opened my eyes and saw Tevye's music box on my own bureau. *First come, first served*. I closed my eyes again and tried to dream another beautiful dream, about a little girl who had all of her grandparents in the world, and whose life was so new that she didn't have to try to remember anything.